© Text and illustrations: Patrícia Assunção

Original title: El mundo de César
Translator: Jane McGrath

ISBN: 978-84-09-21568-3

Any resemblance to reality is not pure coincidence...

INTRODUCTION

Oscar, a salt and pepper miniature schnauzer, was Patri and Félix's first dog. He was the perfect pooch: well behaved, faithful, affectionate, obedient, quiet... He let out his first timid little bark at 18 months. When he died after a sudden bout of cancer at just 10 years old, it was a cruel blow to this family of three.

After mourning for less than a year, Patri and Félix crossed paths with a six-week-old dachshund. He was the last of his litter and was having trouble finding suitable owners. They couldn't resist this doe-eyed creature with stumpy legs.

Caesar barked for the first time when he was two months old, with more decibels than a German shepherd, making his owners think there was another dog in the house. This was their new "faithful" four-legged companion: a dog who turned out to be bossy, selfish, narcissistic, domineering, self-serving, demanding, temperamental, cunning, and a long list of similar adjectives.

Patri and Félix always said that if Caesar had been their first dog, they'd never have had Oscar... but without Caesar and his feisty nature, this book about life with an irresistible canine who charms everyone he meets would never have been written.

Hopefully this illustrated tale will ring a few bells, amuse you, and bring a smile to your face. You might even feel the tenderness, affection and love (and desperation and helplessness) that only someone who's shared their life with a dachshund will understand...

This book is dedicated to all pets (dogs, cats, birds, turtles...) and other animals, wishing them a decent life free from harm.

CONTENTS

31. Incognito
32. Bravery
33. Dropping a log
34. New look
35. New flavour
36. Boredom
37. Heaven
38. Long body
39. Plants
40. Alter ego
41. Hail Caesar
42. Ice cream
43. Pressure
44. Prewash
45. Rain
46. Guard dog
47. Something's in the air
48. Granny
49. Packing
50. Enemy No. 2
51. Revenge
52. Fish
53. Fishing
54. Watchdog
55. Not fishing
56. Titanic
57. The igloo
58. Jumpin' Jack Flash
59. Lumbago tending towards hernia
60. Adapted house
61. Bad taste
62. Old age

1. The beginning

Caesar was born on 1 July 2010, the only male in a litter of seven. Before long, all his sisters were strategically placed in the homes of vets and people who could be trusted with the grave responsibility and difficult task of caring for a four-legged friend. Caesar's first prospective owner was ruled out after he was discovered to have dangerous liaisons (foreign citizens known for their consumption of this kind of meat). We picked him up aged two months and he seemed to be a quiet, timid little doggy, but shortly after moving in, he let out a bark worthy of a German shepherd... This dog was going to be trouble!

WOOF

2. The bee

Like any innocent, inquisitive puppy (he'd soon grow out of it), Caesar loved going to the park and chasing insects. One day when he was busy smelling the flowers, a bee, no doubt tired of the intrusion, stung him. After howling to wake the dead, Caesar had an allergic reaction. Being non-practising vets, we rushed him to a friend's clinic. One shot of antihistamine and he was out for the count. A whole glorious afternoon!

ZZZ
ZZZ
ZZZ

3. The bib

Being proud new dog owners (speaking for myself, at least), we (or I) had the bright idea of buying Caesar a top brand, high quality bib from a prestigious pet shop. I was fooled by the marketing. Our "baby" had to be properly dressed! Caesar's reaction to his original gift wasn't what we expected... We bought him two more bibs, each one cheaper than the last, until, distraught, powerless and fed up with him ruthlessly pulling them to bits, we bought him a collar in the first variety store we found... and he loved it! (☹⚡💣✳☠✝) He's still wearing it 10 years later.

50€
30€
10€
3€
50€ + 30€ + 10€ + 3 €

4. Walks

Caesar's very impatient and always wants to do what *he* feels like doing. It's a challenge taking him for walks, because I can never be sure how he'll behave. One thing he hates is having his walk interrupted by humans stopping to chat. What's the point? He objects to any kind of human socialising by barking so loud it's impossible to talk over him. The more I tell him off, the worse he behaves, and I end up giving in to my four-legged dictator. It's a wonder I have any friends.

WOOF
WOOF
WOOF
WOOF
WOOF WOOF
WOOF
WOOF
WOOF WOOF
#

5. Walks 2

Another of Caesar's fascinating behavioural traits when he's out for a walk is barking at every living thing that crosses his path. I tell him off again and again, but he won't stop. I try the tricks I learned from *The Dog Whisperer*, but he just gets worse. I apologise to his victims, and some people are sympathetic and laugh it off: "Don't worry, I've got one just the same". Others are less understanding and use colourful language to suggest I put a muzzle on him, or worse... So why does he do it? It took me a while to understand, but I honestly think he's telling people to get out of his way. It's his path! What right do other creatures have to invade it without his permission? I'm obviously not going to make any friends with this dog around!

6. Dr Jekyll and Mr Hyde

I have to ask myself: Does Caesar behave like this with everyone? Of course not – only when he walks with me! Caesar's a completely different dog when he's out with Félix. He walks quietly by his side, no barking, a model dog... but when he's out with me, it's a different story. He pulls on the lead, barks and leaps around like a fiend. I don't walk Caesar – he walks me.

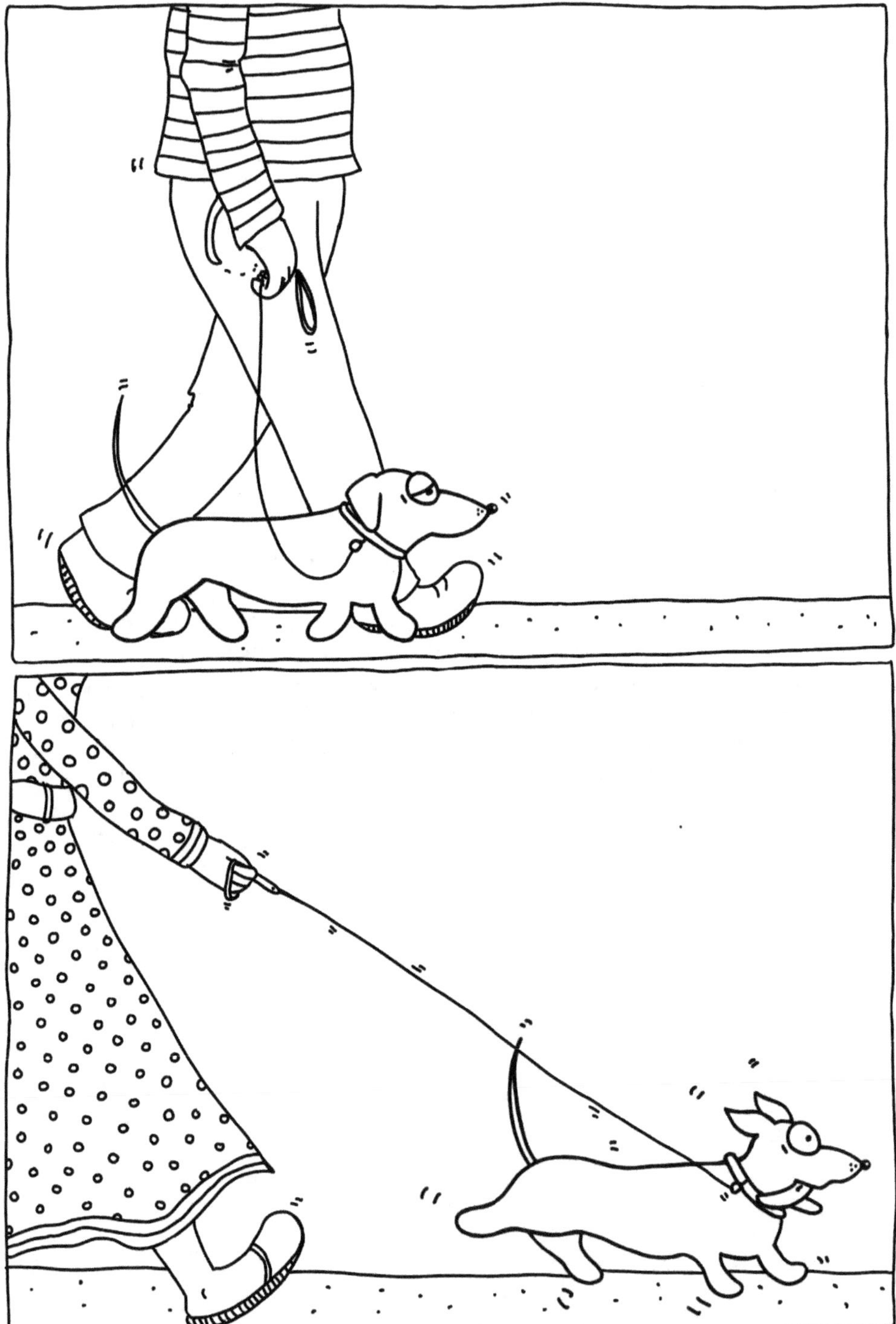

7. Grass sweet grass

One place Caesar loves going for walks is a park near our house... or any park, really. Grass drives him wild. He runs around and rolls in it like there was no tomorrow. Especially if a girl doggy has just walked by and left her scent.

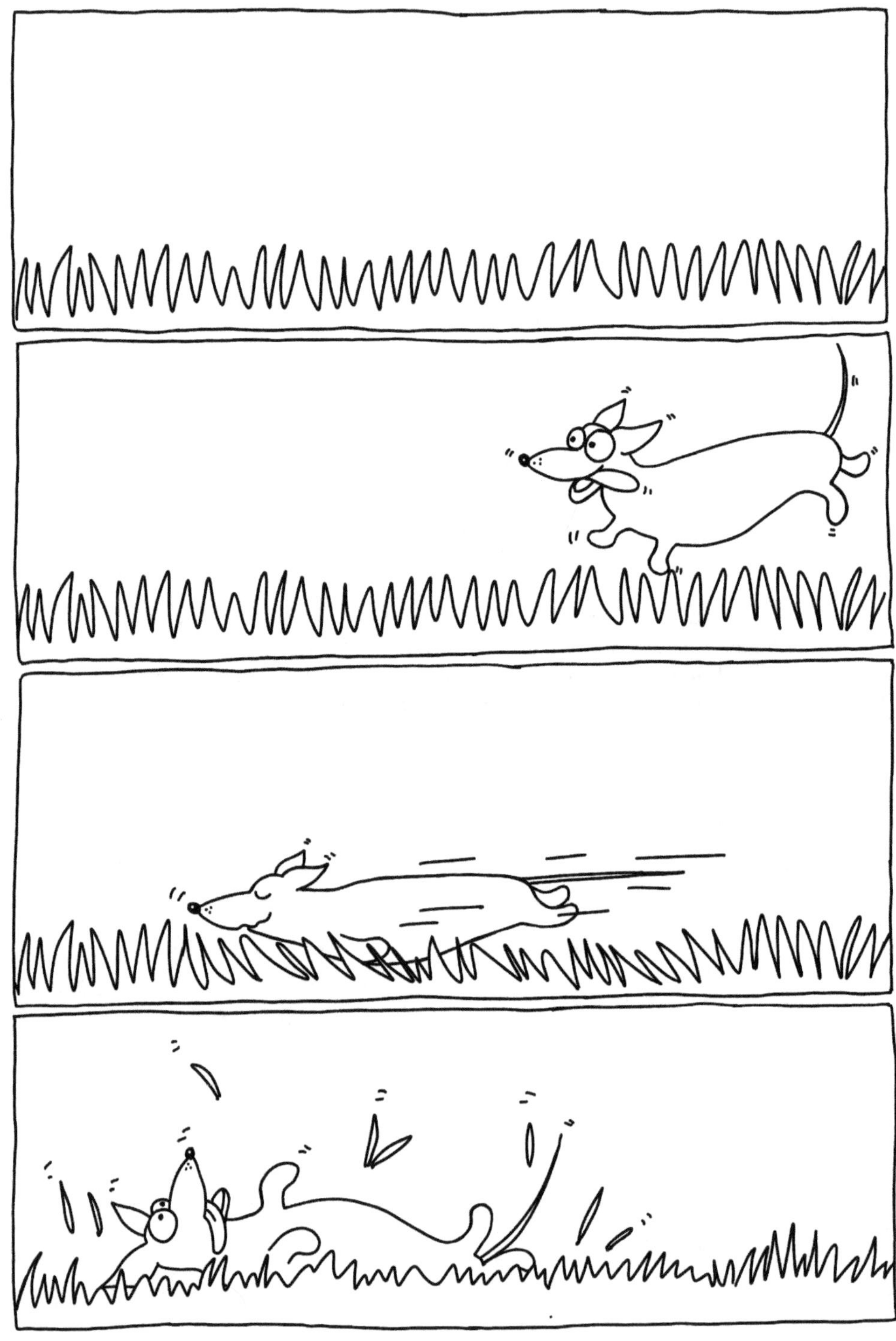

8. Transformation

Grass isn't just for rolling in: Caesar loves eating it, especially fresh shoots that have just pushed through the soil. He walks over it, carefully deciding what to lick and what to eat... he can spend half an hour on this ritual while I wait, patiently or otherwise, for him to finish. No matter how much I call him, he ignores me. Someone from the other side of the world once told me that when dogs eat grass, it's going to rain. While this explanation could be true in a different hemisphere, it doesn't stand up in the Canary Islands. Rather than indicating a change in the weather, when a dog eats grass it's basically because it's a good purgative. Either that or he's bonkers. And here I am spending a fortune on worm treatment and posh dog food... What can I say?

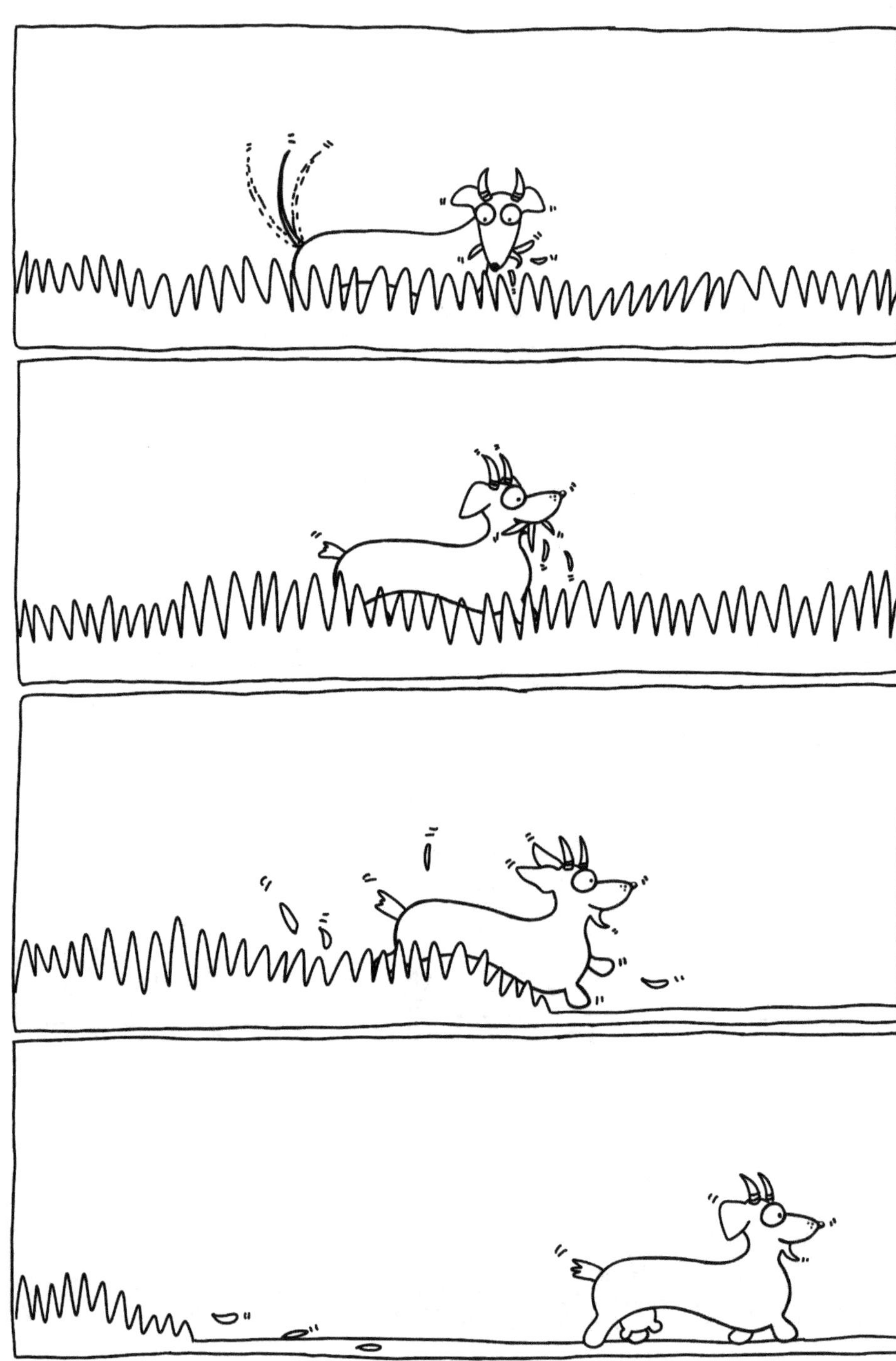

9. What's the book got that I don't have?

Caesar doesn't understand how anything could be more interesting or more important than he is. What's so special about this book thing that it captivates my attention? Reading's a real challenge when Caesar's around. I did my best to read in secret, away from my persistent little friend, until I had no choice but to buy an e-reader. At least I can hold it in one hand and pat Caesar with the other. I've become a multi-tasking dog owner. Necessity was the mother of invention, after all.

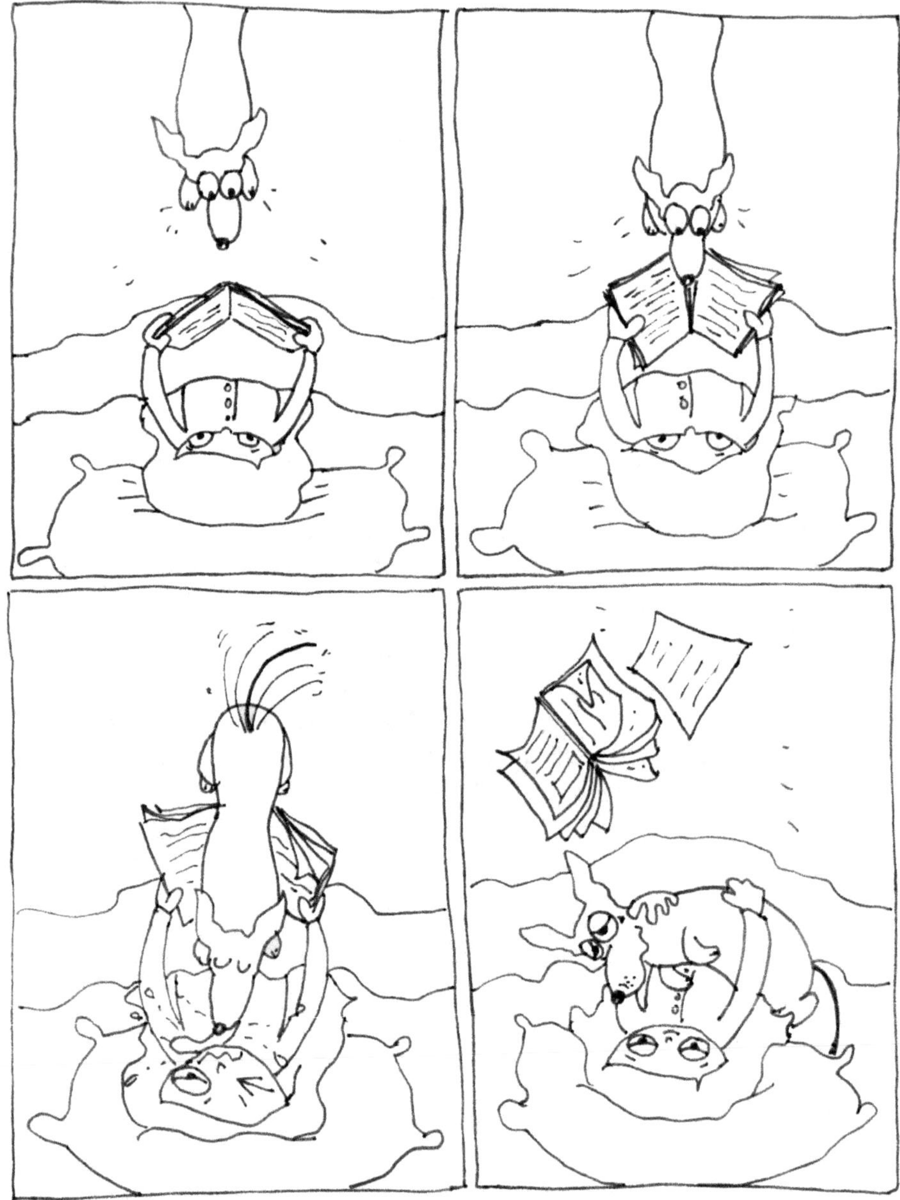

10. Loving licks

The bedtime routine in our house always includes artful smooches and licks when you least expect them... but how can you get angry with those big brown eyes? I try, honestly, but I can't bring myself to fend Caesar off.

Z Z Z Z Z Z Z Z Z Z Z Z Z Z Z

11. Waking up

It's the same story when I wake up. I barely open my eyes or make the slightest move before I'm smothered in artful "loving" licks. It's like washing my face (or having it washed) before I even get out of bed. How decadent! I'm a member of the upper class and I never knew it.

12. 23 Positions in One Night

Like the well-known song by Prince (but without the sexual connotations), Caesar spends the night in at least 23 positions. I've never known a breed of dog that likes sleeping with its rear end sticking out of the sheets. He usually tries to take up the whole bed and I get the feeling he's trying to kick me out, but I could be imagining it. I shouldn't be so quick to think badly of him! Often it's me who wakes up with an arm or a leg hanging out of bed, uncovered and/or totally numb... I have to mount a major offensive to regain part of my sleeping territory. When Caesar's asleep, you can't budge him. He suddenly seems to weigh 100 kg! If I try to move him, he growls... and at that time of night, he's scary.

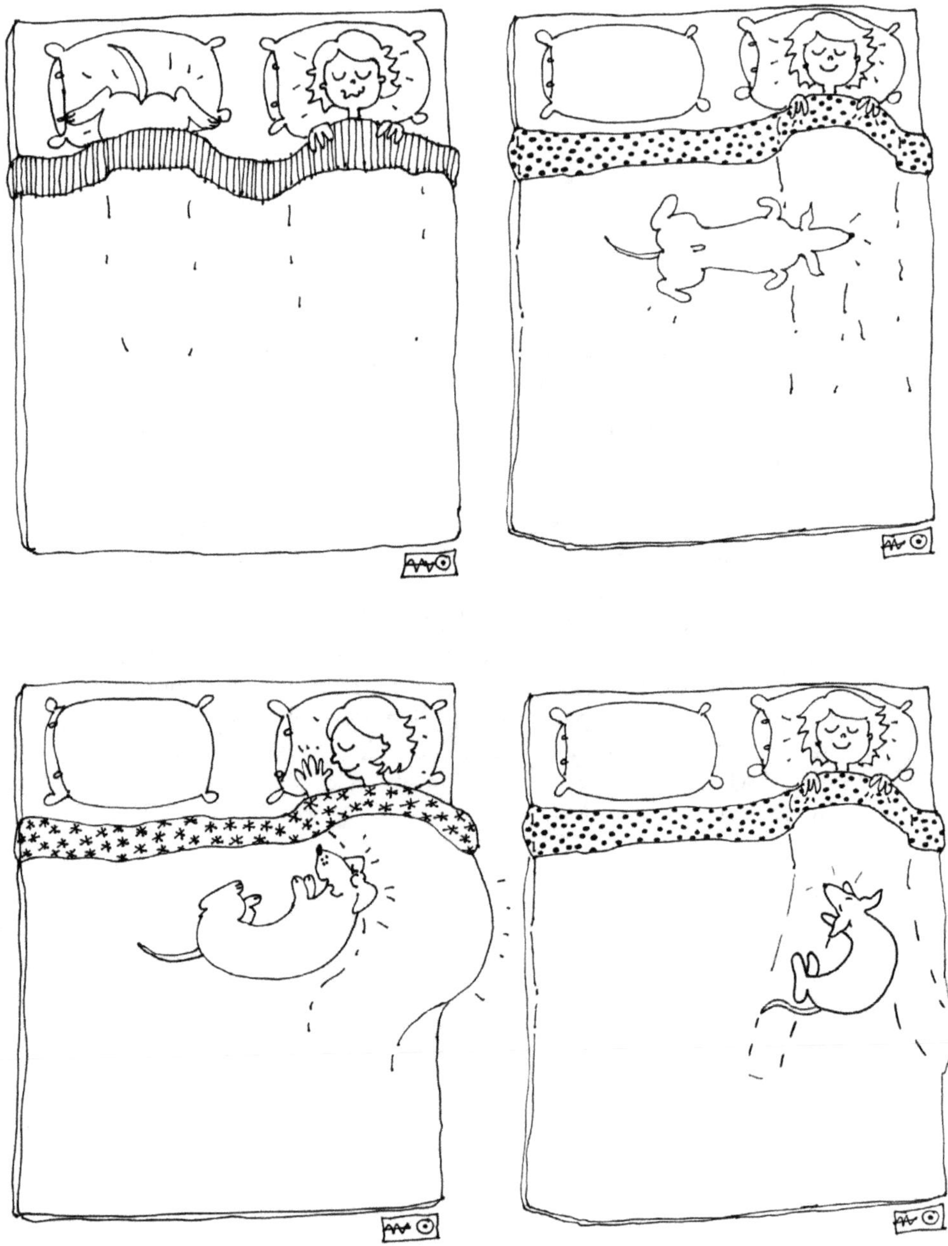

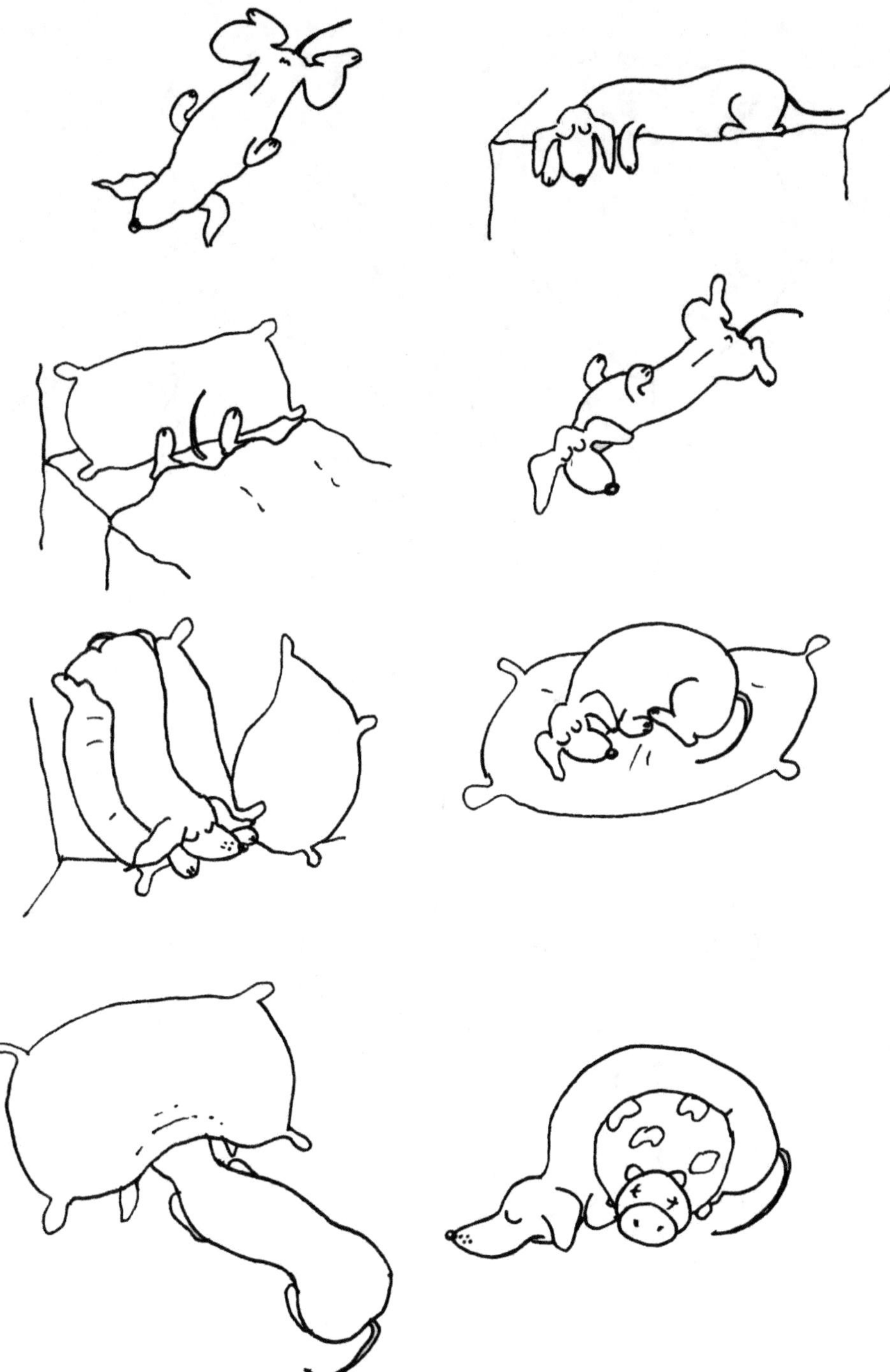

Zzzz

13. Evil mind

Caesar's a dog with a sense of humour, *aka* an evil mind. He loves settling down to sleep with his rear end pointing at my face and letting the odd bit of flatulence escape. Sometimes he sniffs his behind, as if to say "What was that?", but I could swear I've seen him smirk after his apparently unintentional slip.

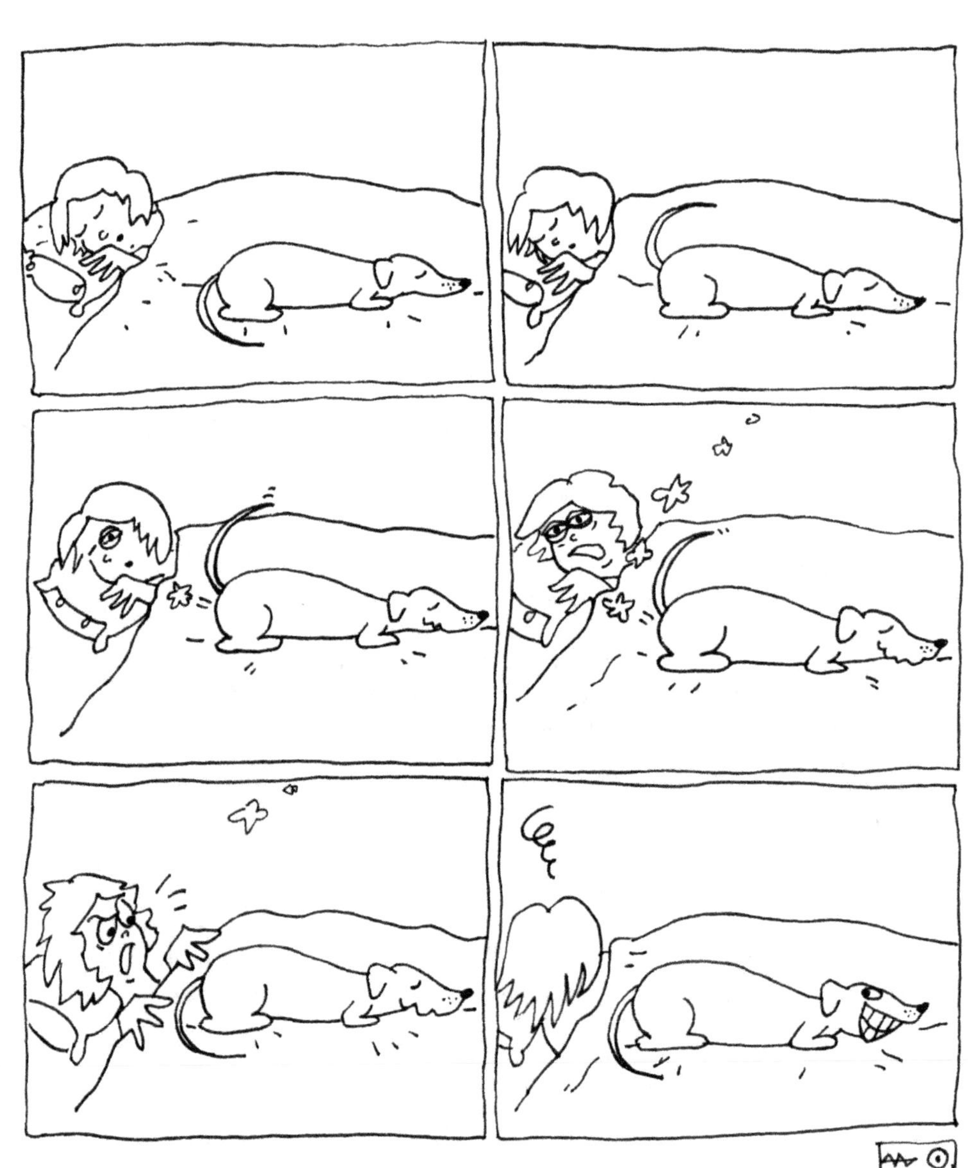

14. Do not disturb

Is there anything sweeter or lovelier than seeing your doggy sleeping peacefully? You feel like smothering him in kisses and cuddles. But do you think a sausage dog will reward you with a loving lick and a fond gaze? No – he's more likely to growl at you like he'll rip your nose off if you keep disturbing his beauty sleep!

Z Z
Z Z
GRRR!!!
Z Z Z

15. Out-of-synch body

That's what dachshunds have: an elongated, oddly proportioned body that often gets the better of them. Caesar's fallen off the sofa loads of times. He sleeps so deeply that he wakes up with a start, has no idea what's happened and barks his head off. Then he forgets all about it and slowly returns to his original position.

zzz
zzz
zzz
z zz
zz
¡GRRR!!
WOOF!!!
¡WOOF!!
zz
zzz
zzz

16. Stretching

Other times Caesar wakes up more gently. He plops off the sofa and does his stretching routine (seriously, I'm not making this up). And then... goes back to sleep.
Not a word of a lie!

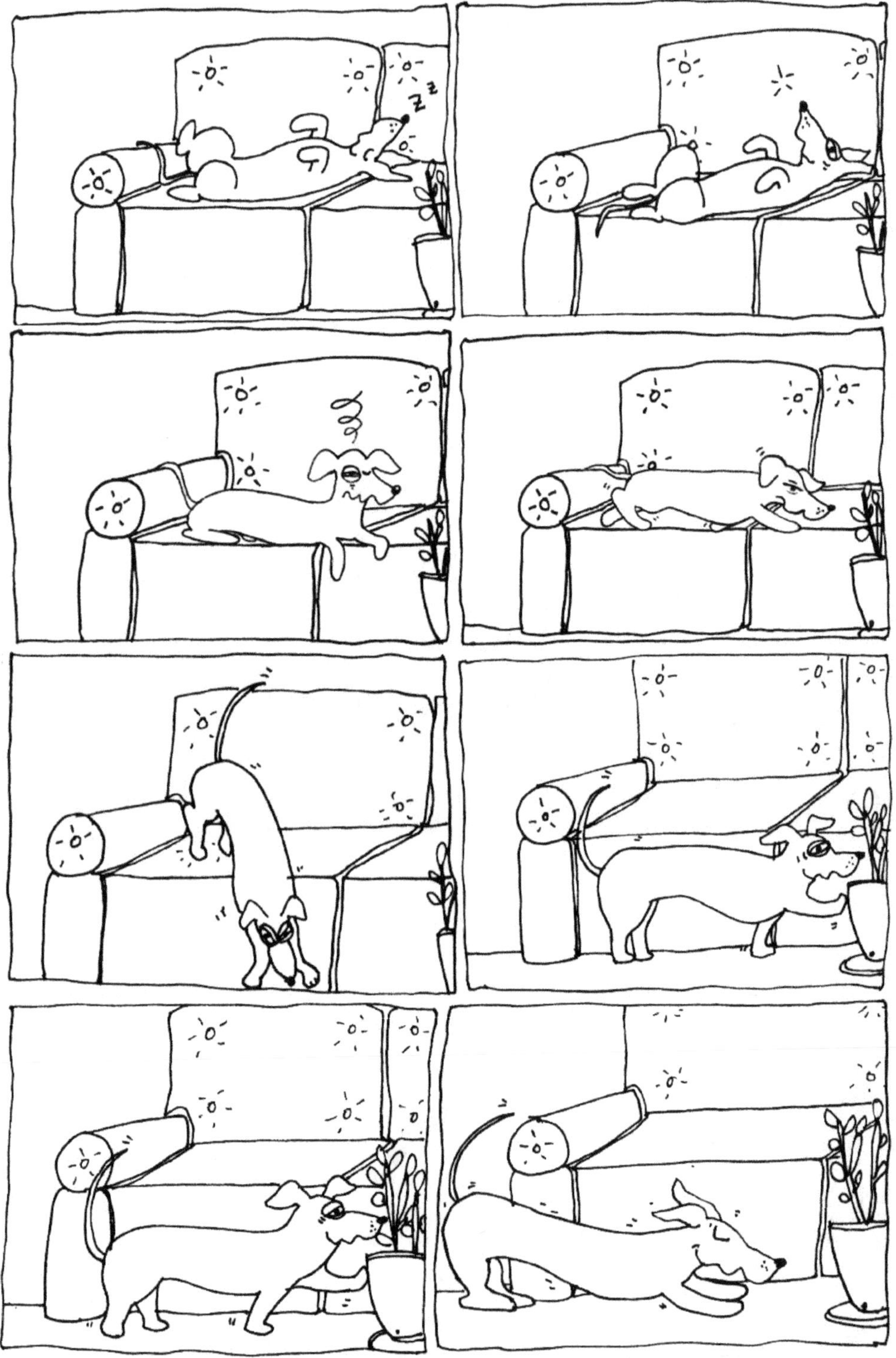

17. Yoga for two

I have my own stretching and yoga routine, and there's nothing Caesar likes more than seeing me on the floor. When I'm on all fours I become his plaything... his favourite toy! He pulls my hair, jumps on top of me, licks me... My stretching session soon becomes *Mission Impossible*.

18. Sweet dreams

When he's asleep, Caesar tosses and turns, whines and barks. I imagine him dreaming about food, dog biscuits, his toys, girl doggies he's chased after and boy doggies he's faced off during the day.

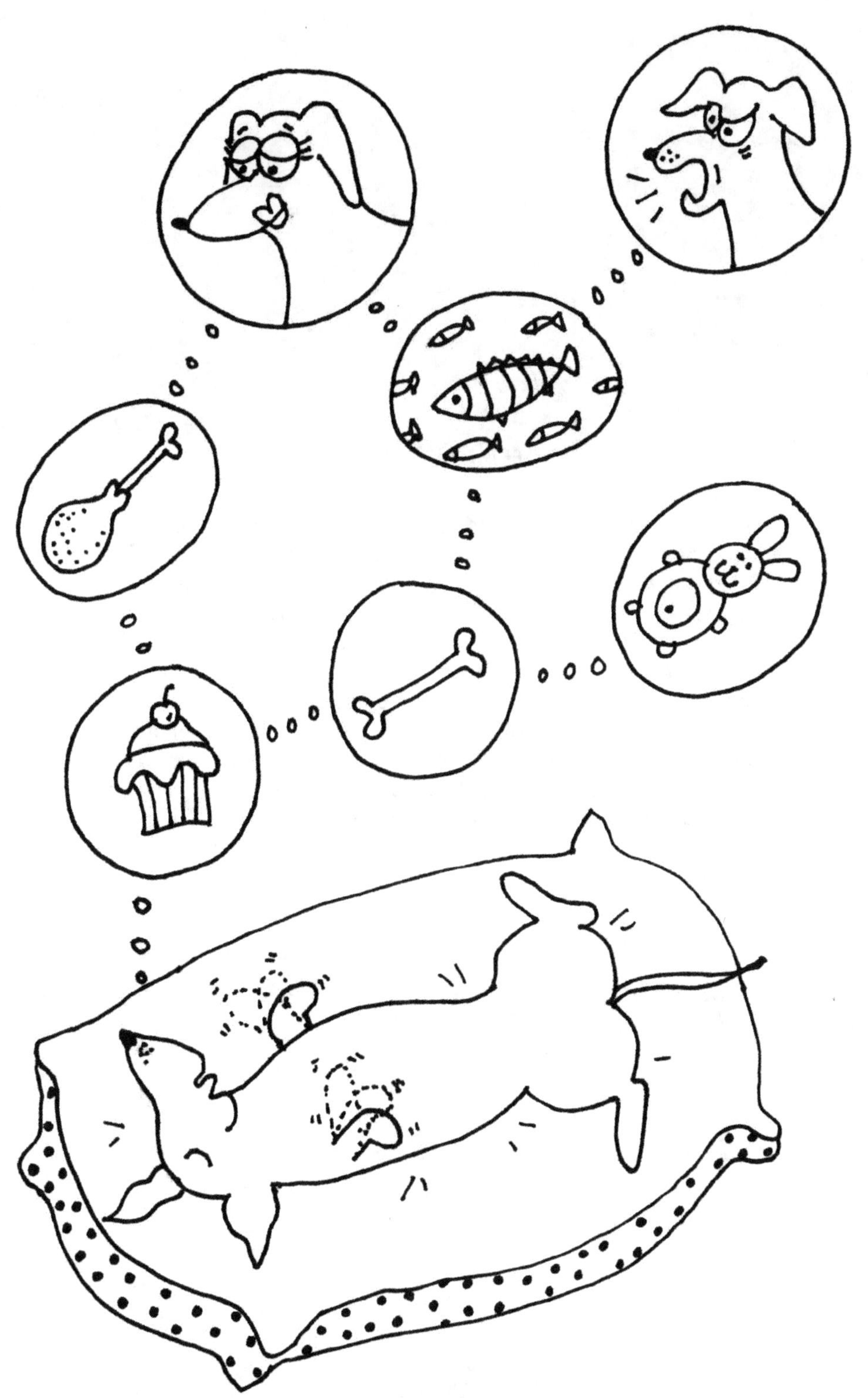

19. Mini morning walk

In our house there's no chance of a lie in at the weekend. Or any other day of the week. At 7.00 o'clock, or even 6.30, Caesar comes to life, wakes me up with a "loving" lick and won't give in until I "decide" to get up and take him out. What's really annoying is that some days he goes out, discovers the grass has been watered, doesn't fancy it and heads in another direction, sees his cat "friend" who likes to chase him and gets a fright, hears the seagulls squawking or some other bird babbling and gets the wind up him, and immediately rushes home, demands his breakfast, then goes back to sleep... I look at the clock, realise it's only 7.10, and I'm tempted to pick Caesar up and launch him through the window.

SQUAWK!
SQUAWK!
SQUAWK!

20. Love is in the air

Caesar isn't known for his good eyesight, but his sense of smell's another matter. Even when he's fast sleep, the sound of the fridge door makes him leap up with his nose firing on all cylinders. When he's out, smells drive him mad, especially the smell of girl doggies... He knows they've been there but he can't see them or find them, and he goes home heartbroken.

AH-HOO!!!

21. Decisions, decisions

While I'm on the subject of Caesar's olfactory system, another smell that drives him wild is food. I have to be really careful about what he picks up on the street... Which begs the question: If he found some food and a girl doggy in the same place, what would he choose?

Note: this is an adults only illustration.

22. Cigarette

Ahem! This never happened, obviously. I'm just playing around with the cliché of the male enjoying a post coital cigarette before he drops off to sleep again.

ZZZZ

23. I need company

By now you'll have realised that Caesar has a friend with benefits... an oversized toy cow (plus a duck, a rabbit, a bear and a crocodile). They were all presents from his maternal human granny, with whom he has a close and long-lasting relationship. The problem is that Caesar likes to do everything in company... even private things. Which is why I suddenly find him mid-act with his face resting on my leg.

24. Errata

Caesar's never used me sexually... it's just my imagination running away with me again, taking a bit of artistic licence with the old doggy cliché. Most people have a friend whose dog has tried to get intimate with their leg. I really am Caesar's favourite toy: he spends most of his time climbing on top of me, licking me, scratching me, jumping on me... but the bit about my leg isn't true.

25. The pest

Caesar's a pest and he never gives up... especially when he wants to be patted. He can be very persistent, and when you think he's nodded off and you can stop patting him, he opens his eyes and demands more. You can ignore him all you like, but Caesar has endless patience and always gets what he wants. I'm more likely to fall asleep before he does.

WHINE! WHINE!
WHINE! WHINE! WHINE!
WHINE! WHINE! WHINE! WHINE!
WHINE! WHINE! WHINE! WHINE! WH
WOOF
GRRRR!!!!
ZZZ

26. The test

Caesar likes to try my patience... he knows I always give in. He loves dropping his toys and "asking" me to pick them up. He keeps doing it until I get fed up, swear in a language I didn't know I spoke, tell him off and throw the toy at his head. He sits there quietly watching me, only to start all over again when he thinks I'm in a better mood. He's exasperating!

I know this illustrated tale's getting a bit long, but it's my way of expressing what it's like to do battle with such a pest of a dog.

WHINE! WHINE!
WHINE! WHINE!
WHINE! WHINE!
WHINE! WHINE!
WOOF!
WOOF! WOOF! WHINE! WHINE! WOOF!
WHINE! WHINE! WOOF! WHINE! WOOF!
WHINE! WOOF! WOOF! WHINE!

WHINE!
WHINE!
WHINE!
WHINE!
WHINE!

27. The despot

This is archetypal Caesar... a despot who thinks he's the centre of the universe. I'm sure he has dreams in which I'm his slave and his wishes are my command. Luckily for me, it's just a dream!... Or not! ☹

CESAR

28. Pecking order

By now you'll understand the pecking order in our house. Not that anyone's ever laid down the rules; it's simply a reflection of the diversity of human nature and what a pushover I am when it comes to animals. I've never been this way before. With my other dogs I never felt like I was last in line, and I don't remember treating them any differently. Then again, I've never had such a bossy, domineering, clever dog. Don't think that life will be easier with a small dog!

29. My friend The Cat

Caesar liked cats at first. They intrigued him. He wanted to play with them and hang out with them, until a calico cat stuck its claws into him and Caesar raced off with his heart in his mouth and his pride under foot. His howling was pitiful, like someone who's known betrayal of the worst kind... the betrayal of a best friend. He's been afraid of cats ever since and beats a hasty retreat whenever he sees one.

30. The fraud

Still on the subject of his feline trauma, Caesar's full of
bravado until he comes across a cat... and if he meets more
than one at a time, it really puts the wind up him. He calls
for backup and as soon as he's in a secure zone out of harm's
way, he becomes his usual "plucky" self again.

¡SNIF!
¡SNIF! ¡SNIF!
WOOF! WOOF!
WOOF!
WOOF!
WOOF! WOOF! WOOF!
WOOF! WOOF!
WOOF! WOOF!

31. Incognito

If things get too complicated in the cat world, Caesar's can always go incognito. Here's another example of artistic licence, brought to you by *Little Red Riding Hood.*

32. Bravery

That's Caesar: brave around big dogs when they're on a lead... but what would happen if the lead broke? No more Caesar, probably. I'm sure several dogs would love to try a bite!

33. Dropping a log

It's not easy, or even polite, to talk about these things, but does anyone else have a dog that needs some kind of stimulus, like a tree or a flower, when it does a pooh? I think Caesar likes the idea of getting back to nature. He takes the expression "drop a log" too literally. While he's doing his business, he sniffs at the plants, as if he needs entertainment or something to relax him. Just like us humans when we go to the loo and reach for a magazine, a newspaper, our latest book... although books might be less common, because they have lots of words and aren't very relaxing. Caesar obviously takes after his "mum" on this one.

34. New look

We're well aware that Caesar doesn't like change. He likes a routine with clockwork precision. The slightest change stresses him out and he lets us know. I never thought he'd be so put out by a simple haircut.

35. New flavour

As I said, Caesar's a creature of habit and he doesn't cope well with change. One day I had the bright idea of buying him a new flavour of dog food. It was a new product, recently launched on the market. I thought he'd like it, but I had no idea how wrong I was. Caesar took one sniff and knew it wasn't his usual food. I persevered for three days, thinking that hunger would get the better of him and he'd end up eating it, but as usual, he won. I gave the new food away and went back to his normal brand. My bright idea was expensive!

NEW FLAVOUR
NEW FLAVOUR

36. Boredom

There's nothing worse than a bored Caesar when I'm busy. These opposing states attract each other like magnets. When I'm working on something, Caesar appears out of nowhere, dives in and destroys whatever I'm doing. I blow my top, Caesar looks at me all doe-eyed and, as usual, I forgive him like the pushover I am.

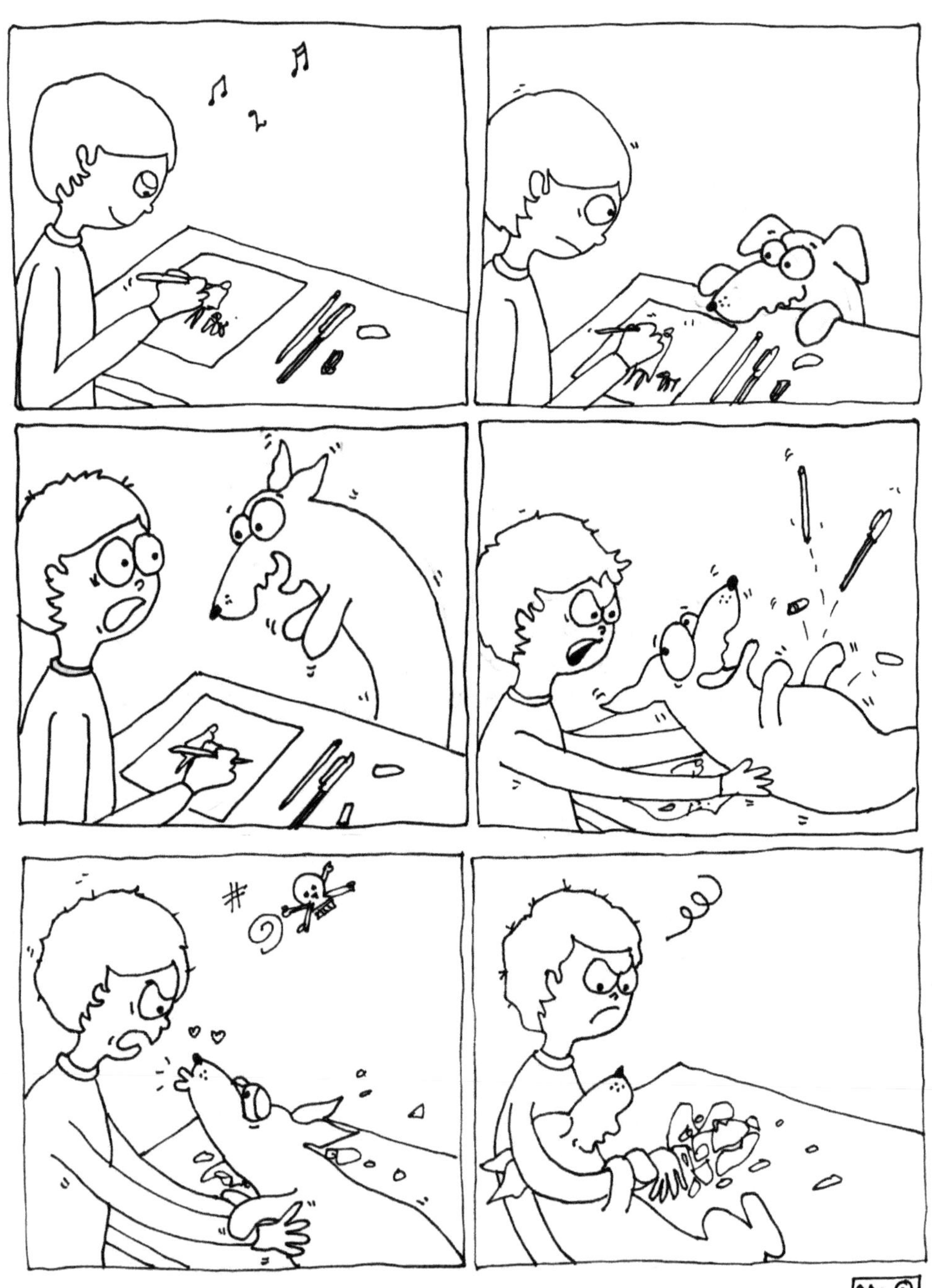

37. Heaven

This is heaven and nothing else comes close... I have my daily stretching session, and Caesar has his daily massage... from a highly qualified masseuse with little choice in the matter. Muggins, of course!

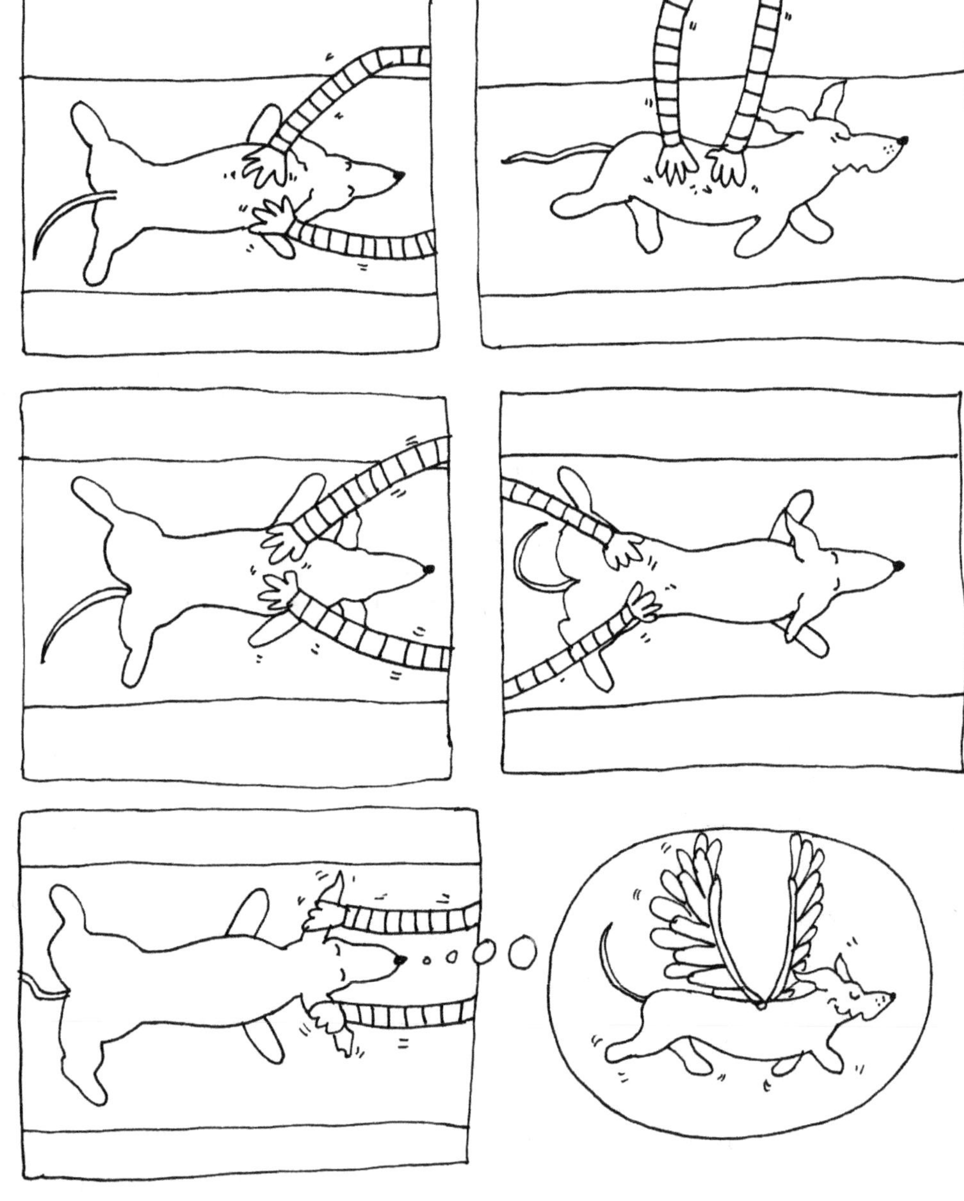

38. Long body

As everyone knows, and as I mentioned, dachshunds have a long, out-of-proportion body. When I'm working at the computer, Caesar always wants to sit next to me. He fitted on my lap perfectly when he was a puppy, but now he's full size I have to put another chair next to mine to take the extra length.

39. Plants

I used to like gardening. Coming home and looking after my plants relaxed me. It was the perfect antidote for a bad day... or a less good day (let's stay positive!). Caesar cottoned on to my devotion and, because he doesn't like having to vie for my affection, he started destroying my beloved plants every time I gave them some attention. Now I have nothing on my terrace except succulents and cactuses.

40. Alter ego

Here the only limit is your imagination. Caesar has many alter egos, or maybe he's all ego. Like the true despot he is, the similarities to monarchs, dictators, generals and similar characters are endless... you just have to let your imagination fly.

K
K

•César•

41. Hail Caesar

Jacobo, a friend of mine who knows my little dictator very well, asked me to draw Caesar as his famous namesake from Ancient Roman. No need to use my imagination: Caesar already plays the part of Caligula. I pictured him lying on his throne surrounded by a court of servile girl and boy doggies.

42. Ice cream

These pictures aren't intended for anyone with a sensitive stomach, so if you're easily grossed out or faint-hearted, you'd better turn the page without looking. This is the ugly truth... Caesar and I always share ice cream, off the same spoon.
You've been warned!

43. Pressure

Because Caesar needs constant attention, he resents any person, object or activity that takes the spotlight off him. How does he let you know? With a lot of physical pressure. First of all he tries to get your attention by gently tapping you with his paw, like a kitten. When that doesn't work, he applies more pressure with his innocent little paw, until the whole weight of his body's behind it. Believe me, it hurts!

44. Prewash

Another thing Caesar loves is rolling around in dirty washing. He adores human smells - the stronger the better. In our house the clothes have a prewash cycle before they even go in the washing machine. Efficient and environmentally friendly!

Z Z
Z
Z

45. Rain

Caesar hates water, especially rainwater, and if it's cold it's even worse. When he has to go out in the rain, he does his business as quickly as possible, on the doorstep if he can. He's definitely a warm-climate dog.

46. Guard dog

When Caesar's asleep, he's out for the count. I've never seen a dog sleep so deeply. A burglar could break in and Caesar wouldn't stir. With Caesar you can forget about that joyful, loving welcome from your dog when you get home... He normally waits on the sofa for me to come and pat him - if he's awake, of course! I wouldn't dare to disturb him.

47. Something's in the air

However, some things can rouse Caesar from the arms of Morpheus, like the smell of food. He springs to life, gets this possessed look and heads for the kitchen hoping for a taste of whatever woke him up. With no ulterior motive, he flashes his winning smile and uses the tricks of the professional flatterer, acting like the most faithful, docile of pets... He'd never win an Oscar.

48. Granny

Caesar loves his human granny. When she comes over, she spoils him rotten, especially with food. Caesar follows her everywhere, knowing that sooner or later a tasty morsel will come his way. When Granny's around, he has eyes only for her and completely ignores us. If Granny comes to stay, he sleeps on her bed. When she leaves, Caesar loses a friend for a while, but he's gained a few kilos that won't be going anywhere soon.

z z z
RING
RING
ENO

49. Packing

Another stressful time for Caesar is when he realises we're going away. He runs about, looks at us, and before we know it, he's made a space for himself in the suitcase. He's a travelling dog!

50. Enemy No. 2

Suitcases are actually his second worst enemy, after calico cats. He looks at them, sniffs them, pushes them over and rolls himself into a ball on top of them, secretly hoping to stop us going away and "abandoning" him with his paternal grandparents.

51. Revenge

I'm really stretching the truth now. Caesar's never done a wee inside, except when he was a puppy and hadn't learned that his three walks a day were for doing his business. But knowing his morbid fear of suitcases, I'm sure Caesar's occasionally considered leaving his mark on them to show his dislike of the ridiculous human pastime of travelling, which is not only unnecessary, but also very bad for canine health.

52. Fish

Why are dogs so interested in rotten fish and other smelly things? Caesar loves rolling in them. Scraps like these have a high fat content and the only way to remove the grime is by bathing him in lots of Fairy washing up liquid (that little drop in the ad doesn't work in these cases). Another thing he loves rolling in is human excrement, so I have to keep a sharp eye out during the local fiestas, when the portaloos are outnumbered by people with urgent business.

53. Fishing

Fishing! Caesar's third greatest love, after food and girl doggies (or vice versa... I'm never sure of the right order). Caesar loves everything about this sport, and he knows that when the fishing rods and other paraphernalia are at the front gate, a fishing trip's about to happen.

54. Watchdog

Caesar's a fisherdog at heart. He's the first to notice there's a fish on the hook, and he's never wrong. He leaps up and barks until the owner of the rod pulls the fish in... and he doesn't stop yapping until it's been returned to the water, because it's mostly recreational fishing - capture and release. Playing, not slaying!

WooF!
WooF!
WooF!

55. Not fishing

We can't always take Caesar boat fishing. Sometimes the boat's too small and it wouldn't be safe, and other times we don't know the boatowner well enough to say "Can we bring our dog? He loves fishing". Sadly, we can't take Caesar these days because of his bad back. He comes boating only if the trip's no more than a couple of hours and the weather's good. Obviously we can't explain that to Caesar, so every time Félix goes fishing (Caesar knows what's up as soon as all the gear comes out), he sulks and waits by the door until Félix comes home with or without a fish, and then perks up again!

WOOF! WOOF!

56. Titanic

That's Caesar when he goes boat fishing... I picture him at the bow, doing a Leonardo DiCaprio in *Titanic*. So far there's been no girl doggy to play Kate Winslet. Just seagulls and fish.

57. The igloo

Our friend Joaquín, who knows a lot about dog behaviour (he's also a vet), gave Caesar an igloo bed. He told us that dachshunds like to hide. Caesar didn't use it much until a year ago, when he began to sit in it often. We think he goes there when he's bored or grumpy (and the older he gets, the more that happens). Without realising it, we put the igloo in a strategic place with views of everything that's going on in the kitchen and the lounge, where we spend most of our time. Caesar has our every move under control from his igloo!

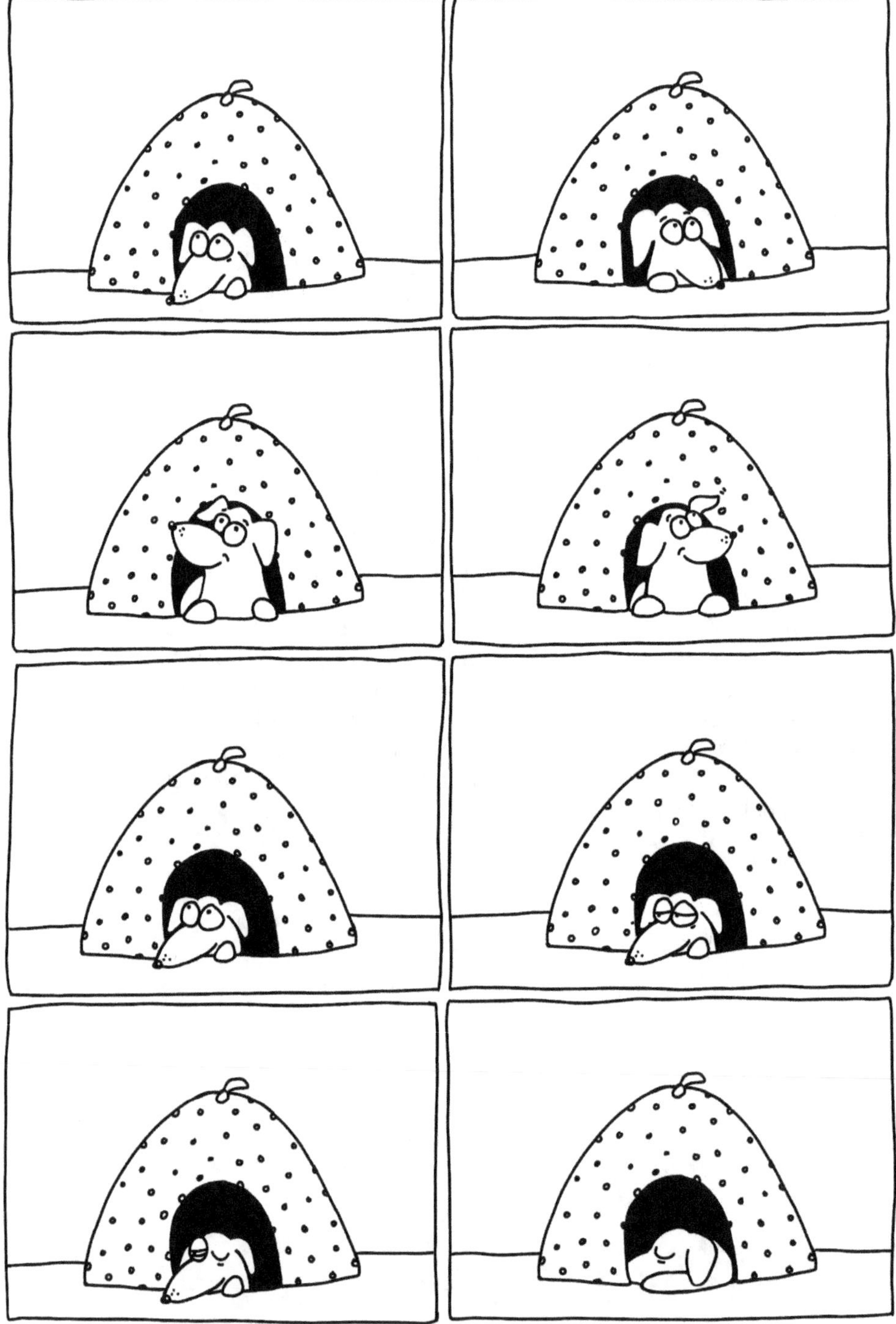

58. Jumpin' Jack Flash

All dogs, especially pure breeds, have typical illnesses or weaknesses. Boxers tend to get tumours, dalmatians have problems with uric acid and blindness, shar peis have trouble with their skin and eyes, and dachshunds, because of their characteristic long body, usually suffer from back trouble. Our friend Joaquín often warned us to make sure Caesar didn't jump about, but like the good friends we are, we took no notice of him. Years later, when Caesar started having back trouble, we had to listen to our wise, cautious friend saying "If only you'd done what I said!"

59. Lumbago tending towards hernia

The reason why we didn't listen to our friend was because Caesar doesn't have the typical dachshund body shape. He's shorter, with good muscles and no excess weight, but, like people who suffer from nerves, all the stress goes to his back. Whenever Caesar's had lumbago it's not because of any unusual movement he's made. He just suddenly starts complaining about the pain and has trouble walking. The treatment for this condition, apart from anti-inflammatories, is normally resting and keeping still when it's acute, except for the basics (eating, drinking or doing his business). But how can you keep a dog still? The recommended solution is to put the dog in a cage when it's home alone, to stop it moving until it recovers. Our Caesar didn't understand, and he made sure we – and the rest of the neighbourhood – knew about it. The cage cost a fortune and we only used it once, because we were afraid the neighbours would revolt and kick us out... and we didn't have the heart to leave Caesar behind bars.

CRACK!!
¡GÑÑI! ¡GÑÑI!
VET
WOOF! WOOF! WOOF!
WOOF!
WOOF! WOOF! WOOF! WOOF! WOOF! WOOF!

60. Adapted house

So what do you do when your dog has back trouble and you have to do everything you can to stop him jumping around? You adapt the house. Joaquín suggested buying a ramp for the sofa, the piece of furniture Caesar uses most. He took a while to learn, but once he got the hang of it and was on the road to recovery (he's still got a bad back but we try to keep it under control), he started to use the ramp, running and jumping like a fiend. The cure was worse than the illness! But the ramp, some light exercise and a good diet (maybe not that last item) have helped keep his back trouble in check. The ramp's become Caesar's best friend in his old age!

61. Bad taste

One of the bad taste jokes a dachshund has to put up with is being called a sausage dog, wiener, hotdog... worst of all, you can get hotdog costumes for them. We've never put Caesar in fancy dress, but I can imagine what he'd do if we tried to. Some dogs like (or have got used to) being dressed up, but Caesar isn't one of them.
Caesar has his pride!

62. Old age

It's not something we like to think about, but unfortunately time passes for animals too, and it's hard to accept that they don't last as long as we do. As the years pass, you see small changes in your four-legged friend. One day you realise he's no longer straining at the lead when you go for a walk, and then suddenly he can't keep up, or has trouble climbing the stairs or avoiding the slightest obstacle in the street, and the hair on his paws and nose has turned grey... They say you have to accept death as part of life. How lovely that sounds, and how difficult it is! For me, Caesar's immortal!

1
5
10
15

Patrícia Assunção was born in Lisbon, Portugal, and has a degree in Veterinary Science. She's lived on Gran Canaria, in the Canary Islands (Spain), for more than 20 years, and dedicates part of her time to drawing and other art forms.

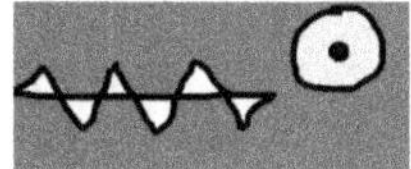